Goosebumps

MONSTER SURVIVAL GUIDE

BY SUSAN LURIE

SCHOLASTIC INC.

Published by Scholastic Inc., *Publishers since 1920.* SCHOLASTIC and associated logos are trademarks
and/or registered trademarks of Scholastic Inc.

ISBN 978-0-545-82126-1

10 9 8 7 6 5 4 3 2 1   15 16 17 18 19

Printed in the U.S.A   40
First printing 2015

Art Direction by Rick DeMonico
Book designed by Heather Barber

CONTENTS

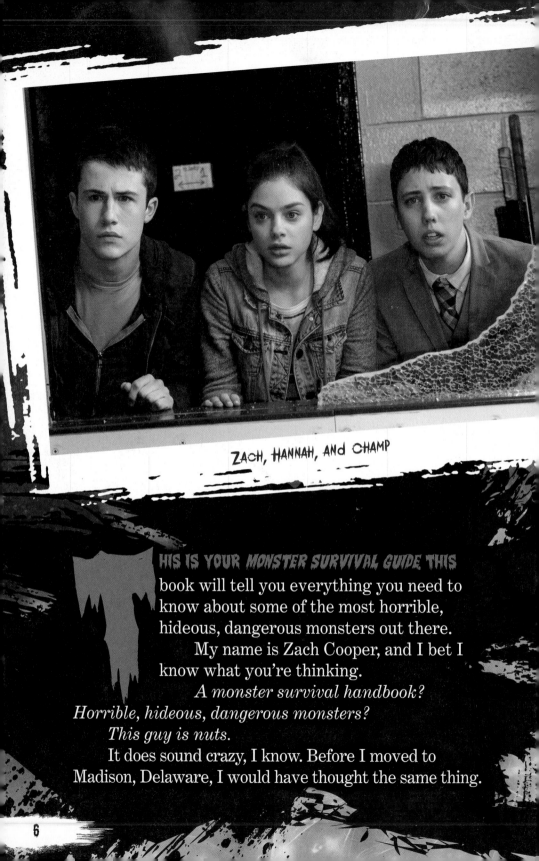

ZACH, HANNAH, AND CHAMP

HIS IS YOUR *MONSTER SURVIVAL GUIDE* THIS book will tell you everything you need to know about some of the most horrible, hideous, dangerous monsters out there.

My name is Zach Cooper, and I bet I know what you're thinking.

A monster survival handbook?
Horrible, hideous, dangerous monsters?
This guy is nuts.

It does sound crazy, I know. Before I moved to Madison, Delaware, I would have thought the same thing.

But you have to believe me. There are monsters out there. Real monsters. They were hidden away in a house right in the middle of my new town.

In the house right next door to me.

The house belonged to a guy named Mr. Shivers. But it turned out Shivers wasn't his real name. He was R.L. Stine, and he wrote scary books filled with all kinds of crazy creatures.

I didn't know anything about Stine or his books, but my friend Champ did.

MR. SHIVERS

SLAPPY

But here's something Champ didn't know: He didn't know the monsters were real. There were bloodthirsty vampires, terrifying ghouls, and an angry mummy. There was a clown named Murder, a praying mantis as big as a jet plane, ten-foot-tall scarecrows, bug-eyed aliens, purple lizard people, and a haunted mask.

There were all kinds of hideous creatures. And then there was Slappy, a ventriloquist dummy—the evilest monster of them all.

All the monsters wanted the same thing.

They wanted us dead.

I don't want you to make the same mistakes Champ, my friend Hannah, and I made.

You need this book.

It could save your life.

Keep it nearby.

It will tell you what these monsters want, their weaknesses, their special powers, and the secrets you need to know to defeat them.

A Monster Survival Guide. *Not so crazy after all, right?*

Right.

So turn the page and start with the Haunted Mask. After that, don't stop—keep going till you reach THE END.

Because here's the thing about monsters—you never know when and where they'll turn up next.

THE HAUNTED MASK

FACE IT—ONE LOOK AT THE HAUNTED MASK, AND YOU
know trouble's ahead.

Its hideous lips gape open. Its mouth is lined with sharp, jagged fangs. Its creepy eyes glow orange.

Touch it if you must. It feels very soft. And surprisingly warm.

You'll be drawn to it.

You'll want to put it on.

But don't even think about it.

Even if it's Halloween.

Especially if it's Halloween.

In *Goosebumps: The Haunted Mask*, Carly Beth Caldwell discovered the mask isn't just an ordinary mask. It was a real face mad scientists created in a lab along with other faces.

All pretty faces ... until they left the lab and turned gruesome.

If you put the mask on, you'll

"I'M COMING FOR YOU."

find out what Carly Beth already knows. It will grow tighter and tighter. It will meld with your skin, and soon you won't be able to tell where the mask ends and your face begins.

Slip it over your head and see what happens. Your voice will turn gruff, and you'll become ANGRY. VIOLENT. WICKED. That hideous face, that new personality, will be YOU.

The Haunted Mask won't quit until it controls you. Until it fills you with its evil.

And remember, one size fits all . . .

KNOW YOUR MONSTER

HOMETOWN: Somewhere near Walnut Avenue Middle School

HOW TO DEFEAT IT: A symbol of love. The mask's evil will wither in love's presence.

FAVORITE SONG: "I've Got You Under My Skin"

LAST SEEN: Madison High bathroom, checking out its killer looks

ALSO SEEN IN: *Goosebumps HorrorLand: Scream of the Haunted Mask* and *Goosebumps Most Wanted: The Haunted Mask*

THE WEREWOLF OF FEVER SWAMP

THE MOON IS FULL.

The air is heavy and wet, and it's hard to breathe.

The dewy grass gleams silver in the pale moonlight.

It's midnight in Fever Swamp—and you hear a howl.

Not a dog.

Not a wolf.

A howl of agony.

Almost human, but not quite.

It's the creature from *Goosebumps: The Werewolf of Fever Swamp*.

The werewolf of Fever Swamp is fierce and fast. Before he attacks, his dark eyes take on an eerie glow. His snout twitches. Then he opens wide to reveal two rows of gleaming teeth. Saliva drips from his long, pointy fangs. Now he's ready for a bite.

What should you do before he attacks?

Bite him first.

That is, if you have a mouth full of silver fillings.

SHHHH! BE VERY, VERY QUIET... AND HOPE HE DOESN'T SMELL yOU.

Silver destroys werewolves. So if you don't have a silver-tipped arrow or a silver sword, go ahead. Take a bite. It will be furry good.

How do you know if you've been bitten by the werewolf of Fever Swamp?

You'll come down with a fever. And you'll start acting really strange. Talking crazy. Making up words. Walking in circles. Dizzy. Hot. Burning up.

Wait.

Is that from the werewolf . . . or is it just Fever Swamp sickness?

Guess you'll have to wait till the full moon to find out.

"THERE'S NO SUCH THING AS A WEREWOLF. UNLESS MAYBE YOU'RE ONE"

KNOW YOUR MONSTER

HOMETOWN: Fever Swamp, Florida

SPECIAL POWER: Can smell kids and horror writers a mile away

WORST MOMENT: When Zach and Hannah tricked him with a rubber steak

LAST SEEN: Madison, Delaware, Amusement Park

THE ABOMINABLE SNOWMAN OF PASADENA

"ANYONE WHO GOES AFTER HIM, NEVER COMES BACK."

MESS WITH THIS ICE...AND YOU'LL PAY THE PRICE.

This titan of the tundra stands upright like a human. His body is thick and powerful and covered with fur. His fur-covered hands are as big as baseball gloves.

Legend says he likes kids. For lunch. But before he eats you, he'll build a nice campfire—he doesn't like his kids raw.

When he's not hunting humans, Mr. Frosty hangs out in his cave, encased in a solid block of ice. That's where Jordan Black and his sister, Nicole, first set eyes on him in *Goosebumps: The Abominable Snowman of Pasadena*. Five of Jordan's shoes could fit in one footprint of this mighty beast. But Jordan thought he was safe. The beast was frozen solid after all.

YUM! THE SNOWMAN LOVES CANDY!

Don't be fooled the way Jordan was.

With one mighty crack, the snowman will burst free.

Then his black eyes will glitter from his half-human, half-gorilla face.

His pink cheeks will turn bright red.

His huge lips will break into a toothy snarl.

If you're in his cave when this happens, stand very still—until he smiles. Then run!

His razor-sharp teeth are about to meet your tender, tasty skin.

of trail mix.

His favorite snack.

Want to become famous? Want to take his picture and show everyone he's for real? Sorry. He doesn't show up in photos. You'll have to catch him.

How?

Well, he likes to chill out in cold places. Zach and Hannah found him in the local skating rink. And this dude's always hungry, so check out any nearby vending machines.

But if you find him, watch out. One touch of the magic snow from his cave will turn you into a human snow cone.

Forever.

KNOW YOUR MONSTER

HOMETOWN: Somewhere near Iknek, Alaska

BAD NEWS: He can turn you into a human popsicle.

GOOD NEWS: He can defrost you, but . . .

BAD NEWS: . . . he has to hug you to do it.

LAST SEEN: Breaking into Madison High's snack machine

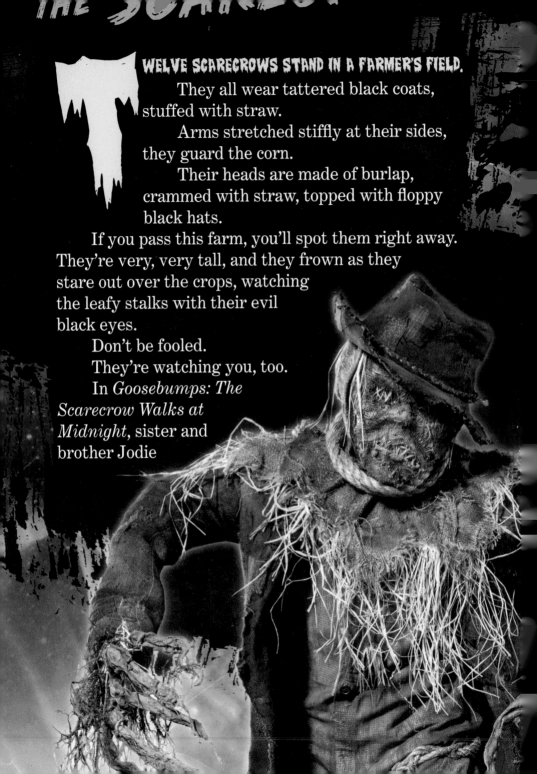

TWELVE SCARECROWS STAND IN A FARMER'S FIELD. They all wear tattered black coats, stuffed with straw.

Arms stretched stiffly at their sides, they guard the corn.

Their heads are made of burlap, crammed with straw, topped with floppy black hats.

If you pass this farm, you'll spot them right away. They're very, very tall, and they frown as they stare out over the crops, watching the leafy stalks with their evil black eyes.

Don't be fooled.

They're watching you, too.

In *Goosebumps: The Scarecrow Walks at Midnight*, sister and brother Jodie and Mark learned that these are no ordinary scarecrows. Their grandparents' farmhand, Stanley, made them. He learned how from *The Book of Superstitions*. The book also taught him how to make them come alive.

If you're on the farm, you'll see them slip off their poles. And you'll hear the sickening sound of straw scraping against straw as they head straight for you.

With their arms outstretched, they'll reach for your neck, wrap their scratchy hands around it, and tighten their grip. Tighten their fingers around your throat. Until you can't breathe.

Or speak.

Or cry for help.

"THEY'RE ALIVE! THEY'RE ALL ALIVE!"

KNOW YOUR MONSTER

HOMETOWN: Two miles from a town called Town

SPECIAL TALENT: They can pull their heads off and walk around without them.

HOW TO DEFEAT THEM: Fire

LAST SEEN: Out in the field—the Madison High football field!

THE LAWN GNOMES

LAWN GNOMES IN YOUR GARDEN.

Three of them, watching over your daisies with their silly little grins and cheerful red hats.

So cute, right?

Well, maybe not.

You take a look at their faces—at those lopsided smiles. *Those happy grins are really creepy, aren't they?* you start to think.

And their eyes. You look closely at them. They're red. Dark red. Not friendly at all.

But they're just small statues, so no big deal, you tell yourself.

Then where did that giggle come from?

It's the middle of the night, and you're staring at the lawn gnomes in your garden. You're out here because you heard giggling. And you're staring at them because no one else is outside.

It's your imagination, you tell yourself—until you step on the grass and see one sneer at you.

Then another one moves his arms. Pulls them back to stretch.

Another bends at the knees.

"Standing so long makes us stiff," the third one says. Then he looks up at you—and they grab you.

WAYS LAWN GNOMES LIKE TO TORMENT HUMANS

10. Pull their hair.

9. Tear their clothes.

8. Stomp on them.

7. Cover the humans in mud.

6. Tickle them.

5. Make the humans bounce.

4. Try to dribble with them.

3. Fold them into squares—they love folding humans.

2. Play tug-of-war to see how far the humans stretch.

1. Use them as trampolines.

THEY MAY LOOK SWEET . . . BUT THEY'RE NOT!

"Look what you did!" The gnomes point to the spot on the lawn where your sneakers trampled the blades of grass.

They twist your arm behind your back.

They're ready to do what they do best—torment humans.

Don't let their size fool you—these mini-men are HUGE trouble. They are superstrong. And they're dangerous. Once they attack, it's hard to stop them.

Zach, Champ, and Hannah know all about that.

They clobbered gnomes with a rolling pin, a frying pan, and a golf club. They stuffed one down the garbage disposal. They caught them in bear traps. They shattered them into hundreds of tiny pieces.

And then, to their horror, they watched the pieces move along the floor. Come together. Re-form.

Cracked but solid, the lawn gnomes were whole again. Even creepier than before. And meaner. A *lot* meaner.

If you have lawn gnomes in your garden and you can't return them to the store, make sure you keep your distance.

Don't play ringtoss with their pointy hats.

Don't pinch their puffy cheeks.

Don't even look at them.

And remember, these little guys hold big grudges.

So whatever you do, KEEP OFF THEIR GRASS.

"CAREFUL. DON'T GET THEM ANGRY."

KNOW YOUR MONSTER

HOMETOWN: The Planet Polovia

SECRET WEAPON #1: Can smell kids and horror writers a mile away

SECRET WEAPON #2: They freeze in bright light.

LAST SEEN: Trying to make mulch out of R.L. Stine

THE CREEPS

ARE YOU A CREEP?

Take this quiz to find out!

PART 1

DO YOU LIKE TO PICK ON YOUNGER KIDS?

TRIP THEM IN THE SCHOOL CAFETERIA WHILE THEY'RE CARRYING PLATES FULL OF SPAGHETTI?

SOAK THEM WITH HOSES ON CAR WASH DAY?

SIT ON THEM UNTIL THEY SING?

If you answered YES to any of these questions, then you are a creep. Go to PART 2 to find out just what kind of creep you are.

PART 2

WHEN YOU ARE ANGRY OR HAPPY, DO YOU START TO TURN PURPLE?

DOES YOUR SKIN BREAK OUT INTO BIG, LUMPY BUMPS?

DOES YOUR FACE STRETCH AND YOUR HAIR RECEDE INTO YOUR PURPLE SKULL?

DOES YOUR TONGUE TURN LONG AND ROPY AND FLICK BETWEEN YOUR JAGGED TEETH?

If you answered YES to any of these questions, then you already know what you are.

You are a MONSTER CREEP!

Ricky Beamer knows what you are, too. He met Creeps just like you in *Goosebumps: Calling All Creeps!*

So stop reading. This isn't for you.

Now, for all you non-monster Creeps, here's what to do if you meet the real thing.

Pretend you are their commander.

That's what Ricky Beamer did—and it worked for him.

Well, maybe not exactly. But let's not dwell on that.

CREEPERS
GONNA
CREEP . . .

Pretend you are their leader until you can escape. It works every time.

Okay, almost every time.

And definitely not if you're a squirrel. (But you're not, are you?)

If you're a squirrel, they'll swallow you whole without chewing.

Except if you're a little dry.

They don't like their squirrels dry—or with the skin on.

Here's something important you should know. The Creeps are on a mission. They want to turn all kids into Creeps. So command them. Give them orders to keep them busy. Then order yourself to get away as quickly as you can.

Unless you WANT to be their leader.

Are you a good leader?

Wait for our next quiz to find out.

KNOW YOUR MONSTER

HOMETOWN: A planet somewhere near Harding Middle School

THEIR MISSION: To hide their strange-tasting Identity Seeds in human food

WHY: Identity Seeds turn humans into Creeps.

LAST SEEN: Baking special Identity Seed cookies for Zach and Champ

THE MUGLANI

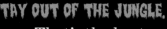

STAY OUT OF THE JUNGLE.
That's the best way to escape the evil magic of the Muglani.

Now you tell me?

Is that what you just said?

Never mind then. Just read this quickly.

The Muglani are a tribe of medicine men. If you think that doesn't sound too bad, that's too bad. Because they're also known as witch doctors—and they don't like humans.

So here's what to watch out for:

1. Do NOT eat the sweet jungle fruit. The Muglani put a spell on it. One bite, and it will turn you into some kind of mutant creature. The last kid to eat the fruit turned into a walking fish. No

KNOW YOUR MONSTER

HOMETOWN: Amazon jungle

MUTANT CREATURE CURE: Steal some magic Muglani powder. Sprinkle it on your head.

WARNING: Don't let them catch you—or you won't have a head to sprinkle it on.

LAST SEEN: Buying Zach a new XX-SMALL baseball cap

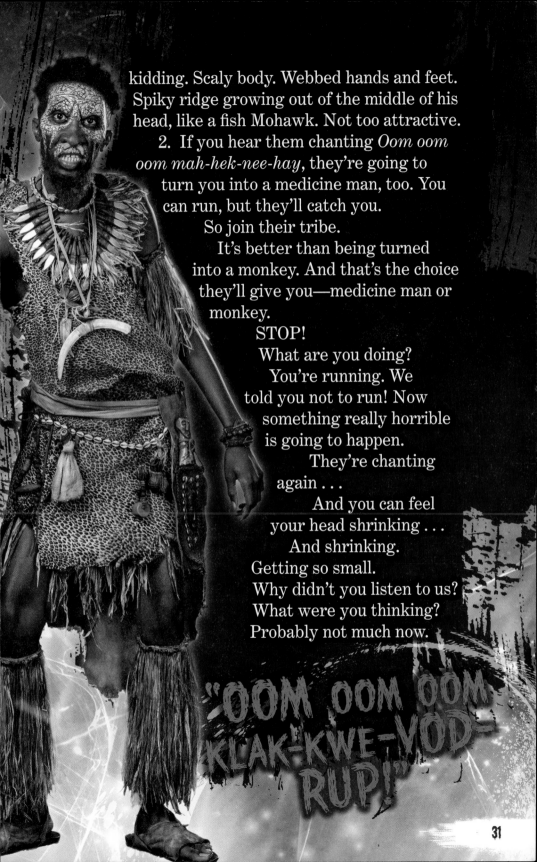

kidding. Scaly body. Webbed hands and feet.
Spiky ridge growing out of the middle of his
head, like a fish Mohawk. Not too attractive.

2. If you hear them chanting *Oom oom
oom mah-hek-nee-hay*, they're going to
turn you into a medicine man, too. You
can run, but they'll catch you.

So join their tribe.

It's better than being turned
into a monkey. And that's the choice
they'll give you—medicine man or
monkey.

STOP!

What are you doing?
You're running. We
told you not to run! Now
something really horrible
is going to happen.

They're chanting
again . . .

And you can feel
your head shrinking . . .
And shrinking.
Getting so small.
Why didn't you listen to us?
What were you thinking?
Probably not much now.

"OOM OOM OOM
KLAK-KWE-VOD
RUP!"

THE PRAYING MANTIS

YOU'RE WALKING THROUGH A CAVE. IT'S VERY DARK. And you're all alone.

Suddenly, you hear chirping and chittering. Is it a bat? You hope not. You hate bats.

Chances are, if you're walking through the Cave of the Living Creeps, it's not a bat. But that's bad news for you. Because that means it's a praying mantis.

A giant praying mantis. As in, a fifty-foot-tall giant praying mantis.

When this creature sees you, his back legs will spring forward. His round black eyes will spin around in his shiny silver head.

Then he'll make a strange sucking sound, and you'll hear a splat. That's the sound of the saliva running off his big, fat, gray tongue and landing on the floor.

That's the sound he makes when it's time for dinner.

Then his wiry legs will spring forward.

His stick arms will reach out from his gleaming silver body.

"WHAT IS THAT THING?"

The antennae on the top of his head will twitch. He'll lower his head and head-butt you.

Yes, he has terrible manners—he likes to play with his food before he eats it.

You'll fly across the cave, but he'll get to you in one giant step and snap you up in his long, skinny arms.

Erin Wright and her friend Marty met the giant praying mantis in *Goosebumps: Shocker on Shock Street*. They tried to escape, just the way you're trying now.

Zach, Champ, and Hannah met him, too. He was very hungry that day—he ripped off the roof of their car, trying to get to them.

Now he's making a high, shrill, whistling sound. It's so loud, it hurts, and you have to cover your ears.

What? What's that you're asking? It's hard to hear you over that shrieking.

Oh. You want to know WHY he's making that sound?

That's how he calls his friends.

So you better make him stop before you're outnumbered.

What should you do?

Kill him. Just the way you'd kill any bug.

Step on him.

He'll fall down dead.

But make sure you stomp on him really hard, because this guy's a big, bad bug with a big, bad appetite.

A CLASSIC SCENE OF DESTRUCTION COURTESY OF THE PRAYING MANTIS.

KNOW YOUR MONSTER

HOMETOWN: Shock Street, Los Angeles, California

DISGUSTING HABIT: Spits black globs

SECRET WEAPON: His black globs are hot. They burn and stick like glue.

LAST SEEN: Doing push-ups on the roof of the Madison High gym

THE EXECUTIONER

PLANNING A TRIP TO LONDON, England?

Well, here's a travel tip, and it's a real lifesaver:

Do not visit Terror Tower.

You can roam the castle grounds, but stay away from that tower.

At the top of the tower is the castle's prison—and its torture chamber.

When Sue and Eddie visited the tower in *Goosebumps: A Night in Terror Tower*, they saw all sorts of torture devices there: the rack where they stretched prisoners until their bones popped out of their sockets. The spiked handcuffs. The thumbscrews.

But their blood froze in fright when they met the Executioner.

KNOW YOUR MONSTER

HOMETOWN: Suburbs of London, England

FAVORITE GAME #1: Pretending he's the castle's barber

FAVORITE GAME #2: Flipping coins. Tails, he wins. Heads, you lose.

LAST SEEN: Sharpening his axe in Madison High's workshop

The Executioner is as tall as two grown men and twice as wide. His enormous chest ripples with strength.

He wears a long black cape, and his head is covered with a black hood. He stares out of a black mask, and there is no kindness in his eyes. But don't be frightened by his icy stare. It's his muscular arms and huge hands that you should fear—and the battle-axe that he's wielding in them. The axe that he sharpened just for you.

So take our free tip—stay far away from him. Or it'll cost you your head.

"DID YOU REALLY THINK YOU COULD ESCAPE FROM ME?"

"YOUR BODY IS MINE NOW. I'VE BEEN WAITING SO LONG."

DISTURB OUR REST AT YOUR OWN PERIL.

That's what's written on a tombstone in the Highgrave Cemetery.

So consider yourself warned. The Graveyard Ghouls are quite clear: STAY OUT.

Don't believe in graveyard ghouls?

Okay. Then open the cemetery's rusty gate. Go ahead. Step inside.

First, you see an eerie green mist. It rises over the graves and chills you to the bone.

Then you see strange lights flicker in the distance—or do you? When you blink, they're gone. Was it just your imagination?

Walk deeper into the graveyard, and the mist thickens. It presses against you. Its sour stench fills your nose and throat, and you start to choke.

You're suddenly dizzy. You begin to reel from gravestone to gravestone, and the graves seem to tilt and shift.

And then you hear the moans.

The low moans.

They call out to you.

Soft at first. Then hard and harsh.

"I ... need ... your ... body."

If you're smart, you'll turn and run. Flee as fast as you can.

DEAd BUt NOt BURIEd . . .

You don't want to end up like Spencer Kassimir in *Goosebumps: Attack of the Graveyard Ghouls*. Frank and Buddy, two of the meanest kids in school, thought it would be fun to tie Spencer to a grave. That's when Spencer met the graveyard ghouls.

He saw a man in dirty rags rise up from the grave. His skin hung from his face. His tongue, black from decay, licked his cracked lips. Worms slithered out of his ears. "You're one of us now," he told Spencer.

So get out of there! Don't end up like Spencer.

Uh-oh. Is it too late?

Do you suddenly feel weak? Feel something

pressing down on your head? Something cold and hard?

And now it's pushing. Pushing *into* your head. Moving down your chest and into your arms and legs. Squeezing your chest until you can't breathe.

So painful. It's pushing, pushing, pushing you out.

And then you hear a sharp *RIP*.

Suddenly, you're floating. Floating above your body.

Watching it move without you. Watching helplessly as it walks out of the cemetery on its own.

That's because it doesn't belong to you anymore. It belongs to a graveyard ghoul.

Take one last look at your body as it leaves through the rusted gate, and say good-bye.

Because it's undead and gone.

KNOW YOUR MONSTER

HOMETOWN: Highgrave

HOW TO DEFEAT THEM: Dance! Graveyard ghouls hate dancing. They'll fall down dead again.

FAVORITE T-SHIRT SLOGAN: "Get a Life!"

LAST SEEN: Madison High cafeteria. They're *soooooo* hungry.

PUMPKIN HEADS

IT'S HALLOWEEN AND YOU'RE GOING TRICK-OR-TREATING with your friends. You check yourself out in the mirror. You wish your costume were spookier. Oh, well, next year you'll try to come up with something scarier.

Outside, a wispy cloud snakes across the full moon.

As you head up the path to the first house, you hear a hissing sound behind you.

Then you feel a tap on your shoulder.

You turn around—and gasp.

Two figures loom over you. They wear dark coats that flow to the ground.

Huge pumpkins cover their entire heads.

They have eerie triangular eyes.

You stare into them—and flames shoot out.

You leap back—and they smile at you.

They smile with their creepy, jagged grins—and

KNOW YOUR MONSTER

HOMETOWN: Riverdale

BIG SECRET: Pumpkin Heads don't like candy.

FAVORITE TREAT: Plump humans

LAST SEEN: Picking pumpkins—that will fit over Zach's and Champ's heads!

"HOW ARE WE GOING TO GET AWAY FROM THESE... THESE MONSTERS?!"

fire shoots out between their crooked teeth.

Your legs are shaking, but you approach them—and tug on their pumpkin heads. That's when you discover the truth.

Those pumpkins aren't covering their heads.

Those pumpkins ARE their heads.

What should you do after you stop screaming?

Run! Run as fast as you can.

Lee Winston and Tabitha Weiss met the Pumpkin Heads in *Goosebumps: Attack of the Jack-O'-Lanterns*. They didn't run.

So get going! Stop screaming and run!

You don't want to end up like Lee and Tabitha.

Or maybe you do.

At least you'll never have to worry about a Halloween costume again.

Because the Pumpkin Heads will turn you into a Pumpkin Head, too.

FIFI
THE VAMPIRE DOG

HERE, FIFI. COME HERE, GIRL!

You want to call that precious little dog. Yes, that fluffy white poodle with the pretty pink bows.

If you do, she'll trot right over to you and gently brush her head against your leg.

Then she'll look up and stare adoringly at you. You'll start to pet her, but suddenly something won't seem quite right.

Did you notice her nostrils flare a bit?

Did you see her lip curl slightly?

Don't be crazy, you'll tell yourself. *She's just a harmless toy poodle*. Look at those warm brown eyes. That cute button nose.

You'll lower your hand—and Fifi's gaze will quickly shift.

To stare at your neck.

At your juicy, throbbing vein.

Her eyes will turn bloodred, and she'll let out a menacing growl.

Then she'll open her mouth, and you'll watch in horror as her fangs start to grow.

Zach's aunt Lorraine met Fifi. Lorraine's horoscope that day said, "Prepare yourself for unexpected surprises." But she wasn't prepared to meet a dog like Fifi.

Fifi is a vampire dog.

HER BITE IS WORSE THAN HER BARK.

Fifi wasn't always a vicious, bloodsucking monster. It happened by accident when she chewed through a mysterious plastic packet that came in a kit called RAIL ENA EJ A AAJ. A boy named Gabe and his friend brought it home from a store called Scary Stuff in *Give Yourself Goosebumps: Please Don't Feed the Vampire!*

The packet looked like an ordinary ketchup packet. But ketchup packets don't say AAJ CAN—GAAL ASAU.

Too bad Fifi can't read. She lapped up the bloodred liquid inside.

"Here, Fifi." If you called the dog, she's probably running to you now.

Lunging for your throat.

GRRRRRRRRRRRRR

But even though you know the danger, you're not afraid. You think you can simply bat her away.

But you're wrong. Fifi has superstrength. She'll knock you flat. She'll snarl at you and bare her fangs— and sink them into your delicate skin.

Now you're a vampire, too, and it looks like you have a new pet. And plenty of time to teach her new tricks—like the next hundred years or so.

Fifi is easy to train. She'll do anything for a bowl of nice, warm blood.

KNOW YOUR MONSTER

HOMETOWN: Not far from a store called Scary Stuff

IMPORTANT FACT: You can change Fifi back to a regular dog.

HOW: Feed her the biscuit that comes in the DOG IN A CAN kit.

LAST SEEN: Looking for something to drink at Aunt Lorraine's house

to that booth right over there. You see it—the one bathed in a soft purple light.

It's a fortune-teller's booth. It has glass walls on three sides and no roof. The back is lined with a red curtain. The inside glows with purple light. Red and purple lights blink on and off all around it.

Come a little closer.

See the wooden figure sitting behind the glass? That's the old fortune-teller. She's dressed in red, gold, and black. Gold gypsy coins dangle from her hat. Her lips are painted black. Her cheeks are bright red.

Now that you're closer, you can see the sign above her booth. It says IAAAIA AKKI.

Scary, isn't she?

Still want her to tell you your future?

Okay. Put a quarter in the slot on the side.

That's right. That's the slot.

In a minute, you'll hear a creaking sound, and her eyes will blink. Her head will roll back, then forward. Then, with a loud CLICK, a small white card will slip into her hand. That will be your fortune.

While we wait for her to warm up, you'll want to know a little more about her.

"DON'T BE AFRAID. WE ALL HAVE TO DIE SOMETIME."

Bad things happen when Madame Doom predicts your future. Just ask Jack and Jillian, the Gerard twins. In *Goosebumps HorrorLand: Help! We Have Strange Powers!* she predicted real horror in their futures—and soon they were screaming for their lives.

Sometimes she actually speaks. When Britney Crosby got her fortune, it was blank. "You don't have a future, Britney," she said.

Soon after that, Britney disappeared.

How could a wooden fortune-teller know Britney's name?

Strange, isn't it?

But how about this . . .

When Meg Oliver and her brother, Chris, met Madame Doom, the fortune-teller was actually walking around. She was alive! She gave Meg a doll that looked exactly like Meg. And soon Meg was fighting her living evil double.

KNOW YOUR MONSTER

HOMETOWN: HorrorLand—The scariest theme park on Earth

THE REAL TRUTH: Madame Doom knows all

WEIRDEST MADAME DOOM FORTUNE: Be good to your teeth, and they'll be good to you.

ALSO SEEN: In *Goosebumps HorrorLand* books

LAST SEEN: Predicting your future

Look! Your fortune is ready.
Still want to hear it?
Are you sure?
Don't say we didn't warn you. Madame Doom is never wrong.
Okay. Here goes.
Madame Doom says there's a monster in your future.
Just turn the page.

SHE'S
ONE
SHAdy
LAdy...

THE *BLOB*

BRUM, BRRUUM, BRUMMM, BRUMMM.

That pounding, throbbing beat can mean only one thing.

The Blob.

The Blob is pink and wet and looks like a huge, glistening, thumping human heart. When it moves, it leaves a trail of thick slime behind it.

Throbbing, throbbing, bouncing forward, the thick purple veins at the top of its head bulge and pulse.

The Blob will eat anything in its path. Make that EVERYTHING in its path.

"RUN! THE BLOB MONSTER IS REAL!"

Its tiny black eyes hunt its prey. Then its belly splits open to reveal its mouth, where its huge purple tongue darts from side to side, dripping with thick yellow drool.

Zackie Beauchamp and his friend Alex fought the blob in *Goosebumps: The Blob That Ate Everyone.* They fought the Blob and won. That's because Zackie had special powers.

But you don't.

So watch out for that tongue. It's hot and sticky and it will leap from the Blob's mouth and coil around you.

Then it will tighten. And tighten. And pull you toward its rumbling stomach.

And you'll be gone in . . .

   . . . one . . .

      . . . single . . .

         . . . GULP.

KNOW YOUR MONSTER

HOMETOWN: Norwood Village

FAVORITE FOOD: Police officers

FAVORITE SOUND: BURRRP!

LAST SEEN: Slurping up R.L. Stine

CAPTAIN LONG BEN ONE-LEG

The bones, they crack; the bones, they creep.
The men come alive in the briny deep.
You ended our death, you ended our sleep.
The men come alive in the briny deep.
So come with us, come with the men,
Come meet your fate with Captain Ben.

ARE YOU READY TO MEET YOUR FATE WITH CAPTAIN Ben? They say Captain Ben was so evil, the sea just swallowed him up.

You say you don't care. You want adventure on the high seas. And you want Captain Ben's treasure. You say you'll take your chances.

Well, listen to this, matey, and then let's hear what you have to say.

Captain Ben was the meanest pirate alive. He fed his men to starving rats—just for fun. And now that he's dead, he's not going to be nicer.

How could he be nice when he's dead, you ask?

Well, Captain Ben's ship disappeared into a strange black cloud that mysteriously appeared over the ocean. That was over two hundred years ago, but gone doesn't mean gone for good.

Legend says if you find Ben One-Leg's ship and disturb its watery grave, the captain and his men will

rise up in anger. Rise up to capture and kill you.

Just ask Billy Deep and his sister, Sheena. They woke up the captain and his men in *Goosebumps HorrorLand: Creep from the Deep*.

Billy and Sheena were lucky. They lived to tell the tale. But will you?

Do you still want to meet this monster of a man and his shipmates?

You'll recognize them right away. Their shredded clothes barely cover their rotted bodies. Snails and maggots cling to their scabby scalps. And their bones poke out of their decayed skin, with their eyeballs dangling from their watery sockets.

SWIM AT YOUR OWN RISK.

"BEING DEAD FOR OVER 200 YEARS HAS PUT CAPTAIN BEN IN A VERY BAD MOOD."

To find Captain Ben, just look for the mysterious black cloud. Then sail into it.

And head down . . .

   . . . down . . .

      . . . down . . .

         . . . until you see his sunken ship.

There you go.

You did it. You found the ship—and the treasure.

Uh-oh. Look out behind you.

Too late.

The pirates caught you—and they're chanting again.

You found the treasure. You opened the chest.
Now you're the same as all the rest.
We men are dead. And so are you—
The newest member of Ben's skeleton crew.
Yo, ho, ho!

KNOW YOUR MONSTER

HOMETOWN: At the bottom of the Caribbean Sea

PIRATE SHIP'S NAME: *The Scarlet Skull*

HOW TO ESCAPE: Sail through the black cloud again—it's the only way to return to the land of the living.

LAST SEEN: At Madison High's fall dance, looking for a new left leg

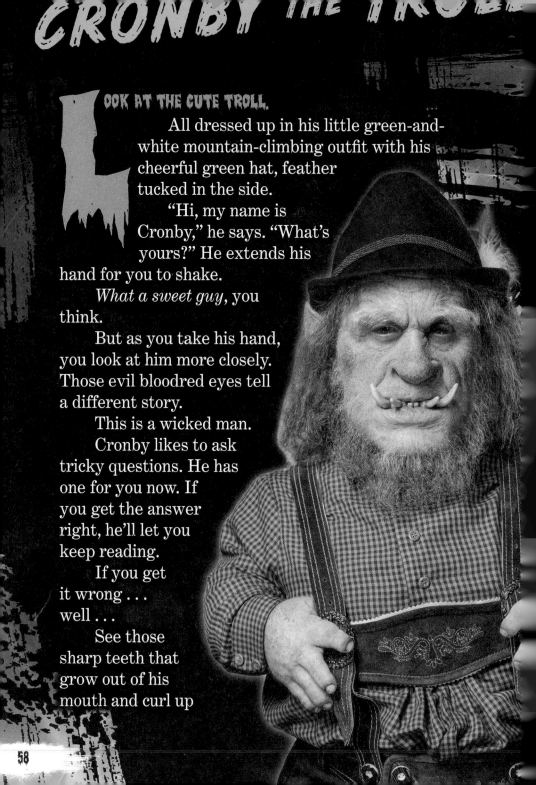

CRONBY THE TROLL

LOOK AT THE CUTE TROLL.

All dressed up in his little green-and-white mountain-climbing outfit with his cheerful green hat, feather tucked in the side.

"Hi, my name is Cronby," he says. "What's yours?" He extends his hand for you to shake.

What a sweet guy, you think.

But as you take his hand, you look at him more closely. Those evil bloodred eyes tell a different story.

This is a wicked man.

Cronby likes to ask tricky questions. He has one for you now. If you get the answer right, he'll let you keep reading.

If you get it wrong . . . well . . .

See those sharp teeth that grow out of his mouth and curl up like little tusks? He really, really likes to use them. You see, he hasn't eaten in twenty years.

And he loves human beings. They're so chewy.

Here's Cronby's question for you:
Why does R.L. Stine like cemeteries?

Did you get it right?
Check below.
How did you do? Is it time to turn the page—or is it time for dinner?

(Answer: Because there are so many plots there!)

"I'M YOUR FRIENDLY NEIGHBORHOOD TROLL."

KNOW YOUR MONSTER

HOMETOWN: A cave in the Jungle of Doom

WARNING: Never look into his bloodred eyes!

SPECIAL POWER: He can make his eyes twirl in his head and hypnotize you. Then he'll eat you.

LAST SEEN: Having a staring contest with Champ

MURDER
THE CLOWN

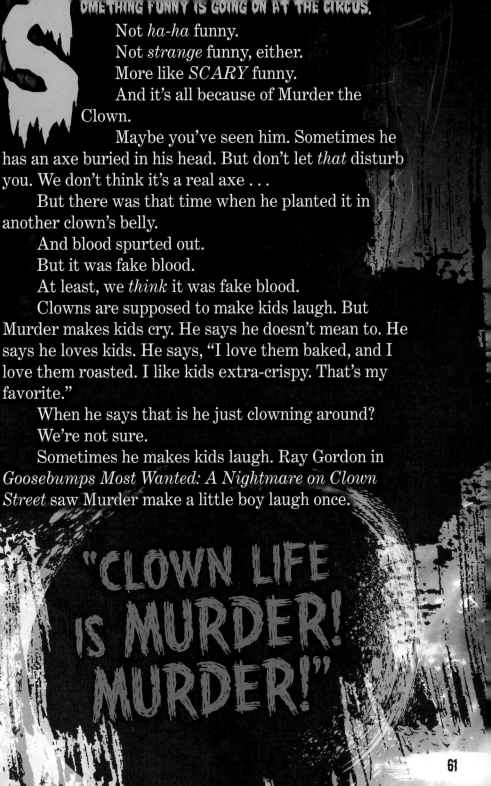

Not *ha-ha* funny.

Not *strange* funny, either.

More like *SCARY* funny.

And it's all because of Murder the Clown.

Maybe you've seen him. Sometimes he has an axe buried in his head. But don't let *that* disturb you. We don't think it's a real axe . . .

But there was that time when he planted it in another clown's belly.

And blood spurted out.

But it was fake blood.

At least, we *think* it was fake blood.

Clowns are supposed to make kids laugh. But Murder makes kids cry. He says he doesn't mean to. He says he loves kids. He says, "I love them baked, and I love them roasted. I like kids extra-crispy. That's my favorite."

When he says that is he just clowning around?

We're not sure.

Sometimes he makes kids laugh. Ray Gordon in *Goosebumps Most Wanted: A Nightmare on Clown Street* saw Murder make a little boy laugh once.

"CLOWN LIFE IS MURDER! MURDER!"

Murder pulled off his big, red clown nose and gave it to the boy.

"Know why I gave you that nose?" he asked.

The kid shook his head.

"Because you smell!" he said.

Never mind. He made that kid cry, too.

And what about that name? What kind of name is *Murder* for a clown?

"People call me Murder the Clown because I murder the audience! I really murder them!" he says.

What does he mean by *that*?

We're not sure about that, either.

So here's some advice.

Stay away from Murder.

Because we think we know what makes this clown happy—he'd love to see you die laughing.

THIS CLOWN MAKES KIDS CRY, NOT LAUGH.

YOU'LL DIE LAUGHING...

KNOW YOUR MONSTER

HOMETOWN: Koko's Klown Academy in Jacksonville, Florida

FAVORITE PHRASE: "Next victim!"

WHAT HE LOVES MOST: Kids! He says they're "yummy!"

ALSO SEEN IN: *Goosebumps HorrorLand* books

LAST SEEN: Madison High's fall dance, looking for a new audience to kill

CUCKOO CLOCK OF DOOM

HERE'S A CUCKOO CLOCK IN R.L. STINE'S BASEMENT that has magical powers.

Legend says if you know its secret, you can use the clock to take you back in time.

We know the secret.

When the yellow cuckoo bird springs out from its little door, grab it. It has the meanest bird face you'll ever see. Don't let it frighten you. Just grab its head. You'll have to be quick. Then twist it around so it faces backward.

That's it.

That's the secret.

Now time will go backward for you.

That's the Cuckoo Clock part.

Wow. You did it.

Time is going backward.

And you're getting younger and younger.

And smaller and smaller and smaller.

Uh-oh. You're getting so small, *you're disappearing.*

Looks like time is running out for you.

That's the Doom part.

THE SNAKE LADY

LISTEN TO THIS. IF YOU FIND YOURSELF AT THE CARNIVAL on the old fairgrounds, do not go to the freak show.

But you want to see the three-headed man and the lady with the long black beard, you say.

Okay. Okay.

Just stay away from the Snake Lady.

She'll be sitting in a prison cell, and she'll slither over to you.

And talk *ssssweeetly*.

"*Pleasssse* help me," she'll say. "I'm being held *prisssoner*. *Pleassse* help me *esssscape*."

You'll find the keys and let her out.

She'll lean in close to you and say, "*Thanksssss*." Then she'll *ssssink* her teeth into your *ssssskin*.

So never ever trust her.

She always lies.

And that's the truth.

THE MUMMY

THE DESERT SANDS OF EGYPT ARE SCORCHING HOT, but stand in the shadow of the pyramid where Prince Khor-Ru's mummified body rests, and you'll notice that it's much, much cooler there. You might even describe it as an eerie chill.

And you'd be right.

Teki Kahru Teki Kahra Teki Khari!

Those are the six ancient words carved on the prince's tomb.

Teki Kahru Teki Kahra Teki Khari!

Deep in the pyramid, you'll find a warning about these words. Repeat them five times, and you will awaken the mummy. He will come to life—and seek vengeance on the person who disturbed his sleep.

Teki Kahru Teki Kahra Teki Khari!

You must never repeat those words.

The tomb of Prince Khor-Ru lies deep within the

KNOW YOUR MONSTER

HOMETOWN: Ancient Egypt

SECRET POWER: Superhuman strength

GREATEST WEAKNESS: Walks very slowly so you can outrun him!

LAST SEEN: Madison High gym, unwinding on the dance floor

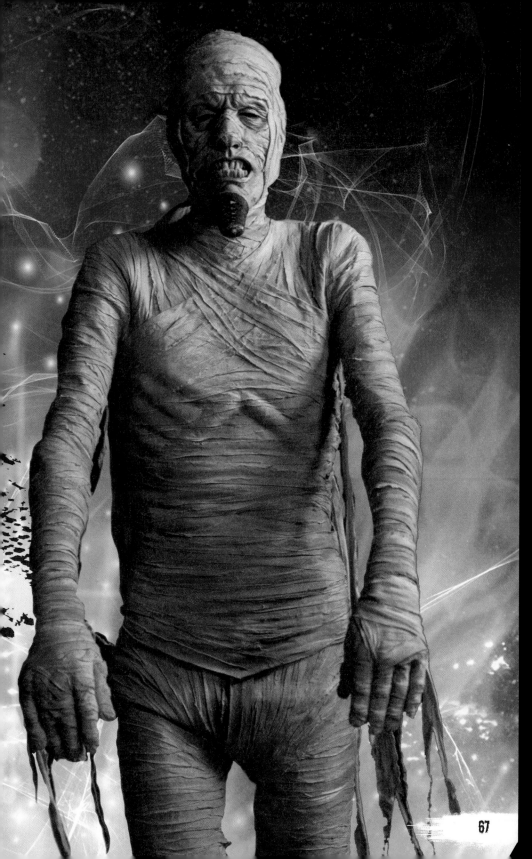

HE'S COMING FOR YOU ... SLOWLY ...

pyramid, protected by hungry scorpions and deadly snakes. It is filled with all sorts of treasures—a lion carved from solid gold, a golden throne, chests of sparkling jewels.

Steal the treasure if you'd like. The prince cares little about his fortune. He asks only that you not awaken him. Do not disturb his eternal rest.

Teki Kahru Teki Kahra Teki Khari!

In *Goosebumps: Return of the Mummy*, Nila, the prince's sister, was searching for those words for centuries.

Nila was a princess by day, but each night she turned into a beetle and crawled inside an amber pendant. The pendant kept her alive for 4,000 years while she searched for a way to awaken her brother. Awaken him so that together, they could rule over Egypt once again.

"LET ME REST IN PEACE."

Teki Kahru Teki Kahra Teki Khari!
Shhhhhh.

Did you just hear something?

A scraping sound—like ancient feet shuffling over cold stone?

And that smell. That horrible odor. The stink of thousands of years.

There he is—the mummy!

His blackened skull pokes out of his yellowed bandages.

His tarred lips part to reveal his black tongue and rotted teeth.

He reaches out to you with his bony yellow fingers.

We repeated those ancient words five times—it was an accident, okay?—but he thinks you did it.

He thinks YOU awakened him.

The mummy shuffles closer. With each step he takes, his ancient bones creak and crack, and he grows angrier about the pain you've caused him.

He lifts his arms and tries to grab you.

Stay calm.

He'll return to sleep—once he has his revenge.

Everyone here is safe.

Everyone except *you.*

COUNT NIGHTWING

You're standing in a dark room. You can't see who is speaking. You take a step toward the voice.

"Come closer," the scratchy voice insists. "Closer, please. I need your help."

The creepy voice sends a chill down your spine.

Don't be afraid, you tell yourself. It's just someone who needs something. Maybe you can help him.

You take a step closer.

The figure moves out of the shadows—and you gasp.

It's a man. Very, very old. Ancient-looking. Over his clothes, he wears a black cape. A high, stiff white collar presses against his pointy chin. His face is pale. Pale as moonlight. And his skin hangs slack over his jutting cheekbones.

You stare at his heavy black eyebrows. Then you raise your eyes to his bald skull with its bulging, throbbing veins.

He takes a step toward you. He wants to ask you a question.

"Are you ready?" he says. "Are you ready to die— then live forever?"

Your heart pounds. You can't speak.

"Well?" he leers at you and crosses his arms, waiting for your answer.

Then he laughs his dry, raspy laugh—and lunges for your neck.

The man is Count Nightwing.

And you were right—he does need something. He's been asleep for a very long time, and he's very, very thirsty.

He's a vampire. He needs your blood.

"I'M SO THIRSTY! I'M SO TERRIBLY— THIRSTY!"

Count Nightwing opens his mouth—and you can't believe what you see. Or more accurately, what you *don't* see. This old vampire is missing his teeth. When your eyes open wide in surprise, he realizes it, too.

While he searches his cape for his fangs, you look behind him.

You see more coffins.

You hear a creak.

The groaning of old wood as the coffin lids creak open.

An arm pokes out of one, a leg out of another.

You turn back to Count Nightwing, and he smiles at you.

"Forgot to put these in." He slips his fangs into his mouth and licks them until they glisten. "Bad memory," he says. "When you live so long, it's hard to remember things."

What should you do? Do what Freddy Martinez did in *Goosebumps: Vampire Breath*.

Run!

Nightwing is so old that if he catches you, he might forget what he wanted.

A DENTIST'S WORST NIGHTMARE...

But who's that standing behind him?

Oh. More vampires. Younger ones. Stronger ones. Thirstier ones.

Guess it's time to answer the question.

Are you ready to die—then live forever?

KNOW YOUR MONSTER

HOMETOWN: Somewhere in the middle of Ohio

POWER SOURCE: Vampire Breath—a green mist that keeps vampires strong, improves their energy, keeps their breath fresh, and restores their memory! Steal it away from them if you can!

HOW TO DEFEAT HIM: Garlic!

LAST SEEN: In the Madison High cafeteria, dodging the garlic mashed potatoes

MUD MONSTERS

DEEP IN THE WOODS, A GOLDEN MOON SHINES DOWN ON Muddy Creek.

If you're walking in the woods tonight, if you're anywhere near Muddy Creek—leave right now. That's what Eddie would do. He went down to the creek when the moon was full in *Goosebumps: You Can't Scare Me!* He would definitely tell you to leave.

And you'd listen to him—unless you decided to see if the legend of Muddy Creek was true.

Long ago, a big storm hit Muddy Creek. A bigger storm than anyone had ever seen.

The creek swelled. The mud rose and buried the poor settlers who lived in huts along the shore. No one helped them escape. The rich townspeople refused to come to their rescue. All the settlers died in that terrible storm.

Legend says that when the moon is full, the settlers rise from their muddy graves. Half dead, half alive, they are monsters now. Mud monsters.

Under the full moon, they lift themselves up from the creek bed. Pull themselves up silently.

"TURN AROUND. TURN AROUND AND START SCREAMING YOUR HEAD OFF."

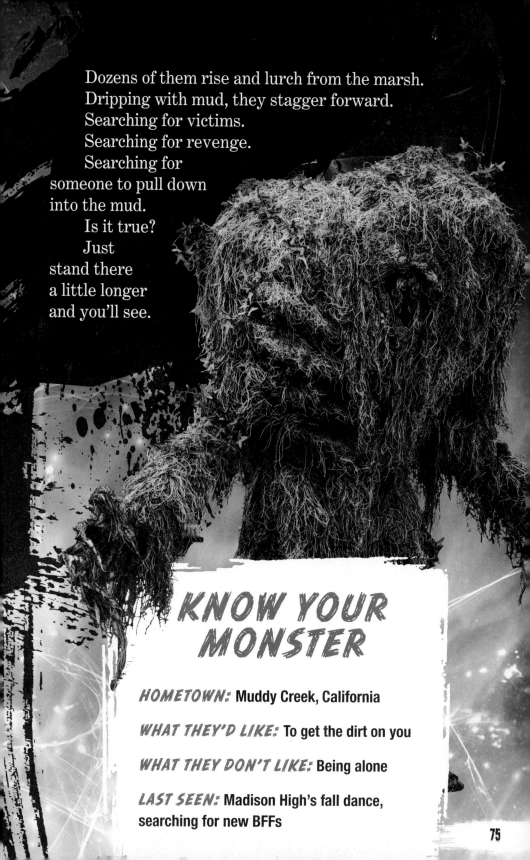

Dozens of them rise and lurch from the marsh.
Dripping with mud, they stagger forward.
Searching for victims.
Searching for revenge.
Searching for
someone to pull down
into the mud.
Is it true?
Just
stand there
a little longer
and you'll see.

KNOW YOUR MONSTER

HOMETOWN: Muddy Creek, California

WHAT THEY'D LIKE: To get the dirt on you

WHAT THEY DON'T LIKE: Being alone

LAST SEEN: Madison High's fall dance, searching for new BFFs

THE INVISIBLE BOY

INVISIBLE BOY SELFIE

he doesn't play nice. Champ can tell you all about it. He leaned into the car and pulled Champ's tie. And he slapped him in the face. Champ didn't know what hit him.

Champ says if you meet this crazy kid, you should yell, "*HELP!*"

Or just stay away from him.

He's got brown hair, and he's kind of cute.

At least, that's what he thinks. But actually, he's nothing to look at.

DISAPPEARANCES CAN BE DEADLY.

THE BODY SQUEEZERS

ALIEN MISSION: FREEZE 'EM AND SQUEEZE 'EM.

When the Body Squeezers first came to Earth, twelve-year-old Jack Archer watched them land. Their blazing orange orbs streaked across the night sky.

Jack watched in terror as one crashed in his neighbor's driveway. Red and yellow sparks exploded from it, like fireworks.

Jack tried to warn everyone about the danger, but no one would listen to him.

At first, Jack didn't think the orbs were dangerous, either. He thought the rocky orb that landed in the driveway was a meteorite.

But then it started to glow with an eerie green light.

And it began to vibrate.

It shook so hard, it cracked open.

And a creature emerged. Small at first, then growing larger.

With a green, slimy body.

Big black eyes.

And razor-sharp teeth.

A bug-eyed alien. A Body Squeezer.

The others followed. They came for new bodies. Bodies that were more advanced than theirs. More highly developed.

Human bodies.

Back then, they fooled everyone.

And they'll fool you, too—because it looks like they just want you for a friend. Like all they want is a friendly hug.

They'll wrap their arms around you—and squeeze. And squeeze. They'll squeeze so hard your eyes will bulge.

Then, as you're fighting to breathe, they'll dig their claws into your back. Their nails will sink in deeper and deeper. You'll feel a painful coldness. It will freeze you in place. That's when they'll make their move.

They'll push themselves into you. Push themselves right into your body.

So stay away from them.

And stay away from humans they've already infected, because they'll try to hug you, too. These humans are easy to spot.

Your first clue: their heads. You'll see tiny green bubbles poking in and out of their ears. That's how you'll know the alien is already inside them.

But that's only if you meet one of the older aliens. Aliens like the ones Jack Archer met.

If you meet one from the new generation, you'll notice it's different. It has sharper teeth and lots more bug eyes. And it doesn't need to sink its nails into you to freeze you. It has a shiny new ray gun to do the job. Plus, it already has a human body.

You're looking at one now?

"WE NEED YOUR BODY."

And since it doesn't need your body, you just stepped a little closer?

And now you're frozen.

Huh? Why did it freeze you?

Because this one really *does* want you for a friend—for one of its alien friends back home.

An alien friend who can't wait to hug you.

KNOW YOUR MONSTER

HOMETOWN: **Planet of the Body Squeezers**

ALIEN IN A HUMAN BODY CLUE #1: **They t-t-t-talk like th-th-th-this.**

ALIEN IN A HUMAN BODY CLUE #2: **They make hissing sounds.**

LAST SEEN: **Looking to hug the student body**

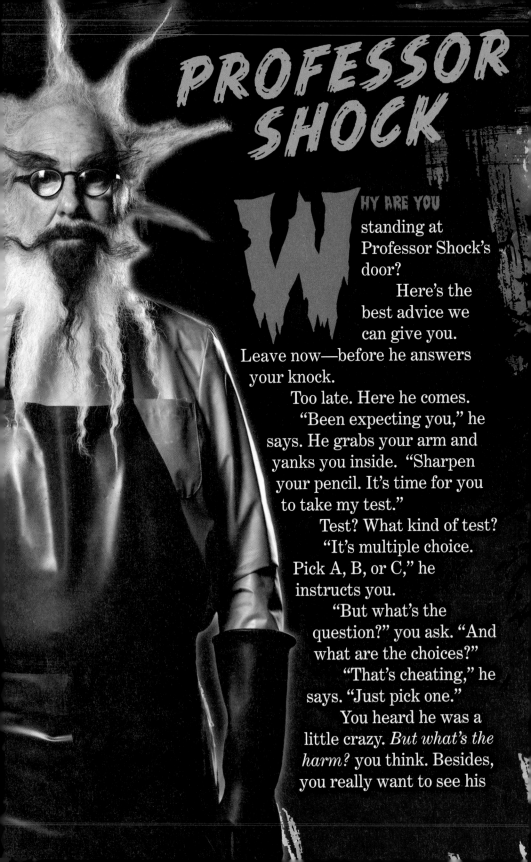

PROFESSOR SHOCK

WHY ARE YOU standing at Professor Shock's door?

Here's the best advice we can give you. Leave now—before he answers your knock.

Too late. Here he comes.

"Been expecting you," he says. He grabs your arm and yanks you inside. "Sharpen your pencil. It's time for you to take my test."

Test? What kind of test?

"It's multiple choice. Pick A, B, or C," he instructs you.

"But what's the question?" you ask. "And what are the choices?"

"That's cheating," he says. "Just pick one."

You heard he was a little crazy. *But what's the harm?* you think. Besides, you really want to see his

"MACHINES ARE MUCH BETTER THAN HUMANS."

awesome inventions. That's why you're here.

You pick C.

"Too bad," he says. "If you picked A, I would have turned you into a cyborg. Same for B. But you picked C. So we play a video game instead."

A video game?

Before you can answer, he pushes you through a green door.

You turn around, and you're looking at the professor through a TV monitor. He's in the room. You're INSIDE the TV.

"How did you do that?" you ask as he takes the game controls and aims a flaming arrow at your nose.

"Class is over. No more questions," he says.

Guess you should have left when you had a chance.

That'll teach you a lesson.

KNOW YOUR MONSTER

HOMETOWN: That New Part of Town Where Nobody Goes

WARNING #1: He likes to experiment . . .

WARNING #2: . . . on humans!

LAST SEEN: Writing R.L. Stine's new bio: *Cyborg or Human?: It Came From Ohio!*

SLAPPY

HE'S RUDE AND SHREWD WITH A BAAAAD ATTITUDE!
He'll pour blue paint on your sister's bed.
Fling spaghetti on the dining room walls.
Rip your brother's clothes to shreds.
And you'll get blamed.
You'll get blamed for it all—because he'll make it look like you did it.

Then he'll squeeze your hand until you scream in pain. He'll slam his fist into your face.

With his superstrength, he'll throw you down and kick you in the ribs.

And he won't stop. He won't stop any of it until you agree to do everything he says. Until you agree to be his slave.

This dummy is dangerous.

He's evil.

He loves to be bad.

And now he has your help.

How did Slappy get control of you?

You made a big mistake.

You read the ancient words that woke him up.

Karru marri odonna loma karrano.

You read them out loud. Then you saw his red lips twitch.

You saw one eye slowly wink at you.

That's when the terror began.

Zach, Champ, and R.L. Stine know all about that terror.

WHO yOU CALLING dUMMy, dUMMy?

Slappy was out to get them—to destroy them completely.

"Who's the dummy, dummy? You can't get rid of me," he told Stine.

Now he's saying the same thing to you.

Sorry, but he might be right.

He's been thrown down a well.

Locked in a suitcase.

Ground up in a garbage truck.

Locked in a closet.

Tied up in knots.

Stuffed down a sewer . . .

and he always shows up at the kitchen table the

"I GIVE THE ORDERS, SLAVE. YOU WILL OBEY ME."

SLAPPY'S TOP TEN INSULTS

10. You're about as funny as stomach cramps.

9. You smell like something I stepped in on the way over here.

8. Your face looks like something I pulled out of the garbage disposal.

7. I've puked up better food than this.

6. Why don't you put an extra hole in your head and use it for a bowling ball?

5. Your IQ is lower than your belt size.

4. You're pretty. Pretty ugly.

3. That was a great dinner. Remind me to throw up later.

2. You look like some warts I had removed.

1. If I had your face, I'd walk on my hands. Let people see my better half.

It's not hopeless. He can be stopped. But it won't be easy. We heard that he was defeated by Dennis and Rocky. They were dummies, too. Seems like it takes a dummy to stop a dummy.

Wait. R.L. Stine defeated him.

Hmmm.

Guess that would make him one smart dummy.

Do you have what it takes to defeat Slappy?

Are you one smart dummy, too?

SLAPPY WITH HIS BELOVED CREATOR, R.L. STINE.

DON'T DRIVE WITH A DUMMY, NO MATTER HOW SMART HE IS.

KNOW YOUR MONSTER

HOMETOWN: Ancient castle of an evil sorcerer

WHAT SCARES SLAPPY: Termites

WHY HE'S BAD TO THE BONE: He's carved from the wood of a stolen coffin.

ALSO SEEN IN: Goosebumps: Night of the Living Dummy, Goosebumps: Night of the Living Dummy II, Goosebumps: Night of the Living Dummy III, Goosebumps 2000: Bride of the Living Dummy, Goosebumps 2000: Slappy's Nightmare, Goosebumps HorrorLand: Revenge of the Living Dummy, Goosebumps HorrorLand: Slappy New Year!, Goosebumps Most Wanted: Son of Slappy

LAST SEEN: Pretending to be R.L. Stine

THE HAUNTED CAR

THIS IS THE CAR OF YOUR DREAMS.

Deep, shiny blue with a white leather interior. Sleek fenders. Snazzy headlights. Classy. Not a scratch on it.

The engine revs up with a steady roar. POWERFUL.

Open the door. Get behind the wheel. You don't want to?

Actually, you don't have a choice. Because this car will call you. "Go ahead," you'll hear it whisper. "Climb in."

A chill will run down your spine. *Run!* you'll tell yourself. *Get away, now!*

But you're not in control anymore. Your hand will reach out to open the door. You'll try to pull it away. But you won't be able to.

"I DIED IN THIS CAR. AND NOW IT'S YOUR TURN!"

"That's right," you'll hear the whisper again. It's a girl's whisper, soft and cruel. "Come on in."

You'll slip in behind the wheel.

You'll see the dazzling dashboard with its glowing dials. Sweet, you'll think—until you hear the locks click shut.

You'll try to open the doors, but they're stuck.

What's going on? Your heart will start to pound.

And then the air will turn chilly. Then icy. Then freezing. Who turned on the air-conditioning—and why can't you turn it off?

You'll look for the driver's manual, but you won't find one.

Because this car only comes with a small scrap of paper. On it are these words:

I'M EVIL.

In *Goosebumps: The Haunted Car*, Mitchell Moinian thought he knew everything there was to know about cars—until he found himself trapped inside this one with no way out.

You see, this car is haunted by an evil ghost girl, and no one can match her wickedness.

No one except Slappy. That's why this car is his perfect ride, and definitely not yours.

Make no mistake about it. You may be in the driver's seat, but this ghost girl is in control. Your first ride in this car will be your last.

This *is* the car of your dreams—your nightmares.

KNOW YOUR MONSTER

HOMETOWN: Forrest Valley

FAVORITE PHRASE: "I'm evil. I'm so evil."

#1 WISH: Wants a new ghost friend—you

LAST SEEN: Forrest Valley Road with Slappy at the wheel!

ANNIHILATOR 3000

WHAT'S SILVER AND RED AND STARING AT ME *with glowing eyes?*

If you're asking yourself this question, you're already doomed.

Listen carefully. Here's what you should do. Make that what you should NOT do.

Do NOT move.

If you move, this monster will point its finger at you—and a red-hot laser beam will shoot out of it. This laser beam can set your bed on fire, explode your computer, blow up your cat. You get the picture.

Or a cold blue beam might shoot out from its chest. Not much better. This one is icy. It can turn your dog into a pupsicle. Freeze you to death.

What is this doom machine?

It's the Annihilator 3000 robot.

What does it want?

The total destruction of everything that crosses its path.

You know what that means?

It means . . .

this . . .

is . . .

THE END.

CONCLUSION

ZACH HERE. JUST WANTED TO MAKE SURE YOU made it to the end.

Just reading about these monsters was scary, right?

Let me tell you—it was terrifying to fight them for real. But my friends and I did it.

Okay, we had a little help. All right, we had a lot of help.

But you won't need any help.

All you need is this book.

But, Zach, you got rid of them. Why worry? I'm guessing that's what you're thinking now.

Good question.

So here's one last thing you should know about these monsters. They don't like to lose. They always find a way to return—for revenge.

Trust me. They'll be back.